I dedicate this book to Richard, my mother and my son and daughter. I have been truly blessed to have all of you.

I love you forever, Adrienne aka GiGi Banks

To Maya and Sirius, the new additions to the family. Love you both

Tiffany

D1368250

It was early in the morning.
The sun was beaming brightly.

The branches blew
from side to side.

The forest had
a wonderful scent
of wildflowers.

The monkeys swing from tree to tree chattering about food.

The rabbits, frogs, and birds scattered around whispering about food.

The animals in the lake were gossiping about where to find food.

Kayla is a brave, quiet, little seven year old girl who is fascinated with animals. Kayla walked through the woods boldly with Peedy by her side.

Peeby flapped his wings and said, "Let's go home!
Let's go home!" Kayla said, "Be quiet and listen to
those animals. They're talking! Do you hear them?
Can you believe it?" Kayla was amazed.

She put her hands on her hips and
wiggled from side to side, and said
"Leaping lizards that's incredible!"

Let's go sit on the green log over there. So she went and sat on the green log. At that moment, something strange began to happen. The log began to move slowly. Then it started talking. "If you want a ride go to the amusement park. I am not a horse. I'm an alligator, an alligator I am longer than 6 feet, faster than lightning, and my jaws are so strong that I can chew you and that loud bird up!

Now get lost kid!"

Kayla ran and ran
till she came to
a huge mysterious
looking tree.
She was breathing
heavily and said,
"Leap Liz Liz lizards!"

She sat under the tree.
A plump juicy peach
fell on her head.

She picked it up and took a bite.
Then the tree said,

"My fruit is for the animals only."

Kayla dropped the peach,
her eyes became as big
as two apples
She was stunned because
she never had seen
a talking tree.

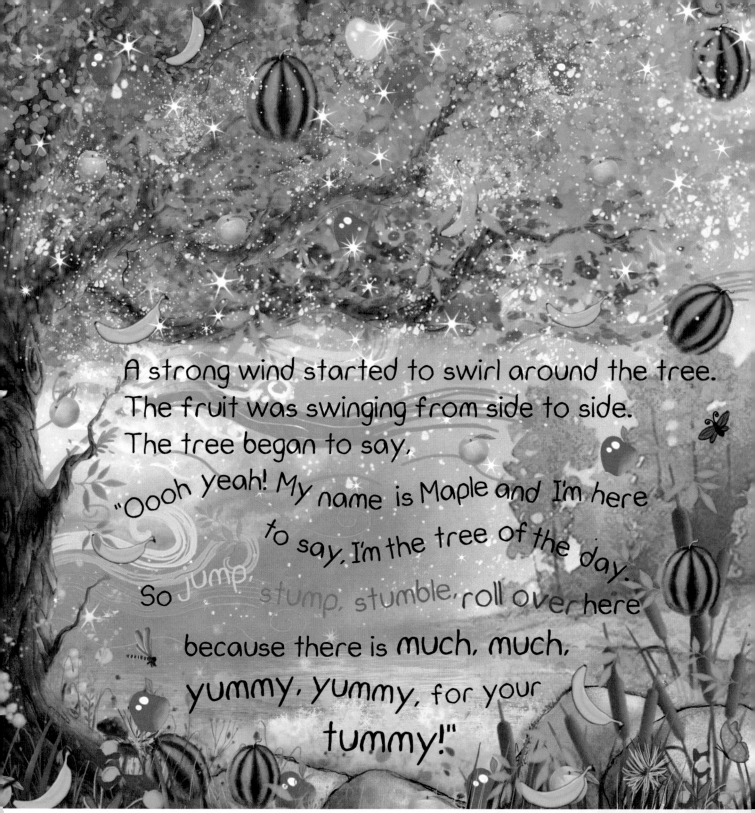

A strong wind started to swirl around the tree.
The fruit was swinging from side to side.
The tree began to say,

"Oooh yeah! My name is Maple and I'm here
to say, I'm the tree of the day.
So jump, stump, stumble, roll over here
because there is much, much,
yummy, yummy, for your
tummy!"

The tree was raining
all types of fruit.

At that moment animals
came from everywhere.

The monkeys were grabbing
honey yellow bananas,

The rabbits were biting
shiny juicy red apples.

Those frogs were biting into
the plump juicy glowing peaches.

The birds nibbling on emerald green grapes.

A silver fox biting on a big ripe
watermelon on the ground.

In the back the squirrels were
grabbing those big delicious nuts.

There was something for everyone.

Kayla walks away from the tree and jumps up into the air. She is so happy to be in the talking forest.

Just then a strong wind came her way.
Feathers were flying all over. Whoosh,
a big eagle landed directly in front of her.

The eagle said,

"Little girl,
what are you doing
here in the forest?
It's dangerous!"

Kayla said,

"I know but I love the animals.
Hey, who taught you to talk?"

The eagle said,

"Then go to the zoo.
The zoo is the place for you.

Now, you asked who taught me to talk?
I open my mouth and the words come out.
I'm an eagle. My eyesight is four times better
than a human with perfect vision.
I'm one of the best flyers in the air."

Then the sly red fox came out.

He walked behind Kayla.

He started talking,

"Hey little girl, that bird looks awful

heavy on the shoulders.

Why don't you let me help you out?

I'll hold him for you."

Peedy said, "Let's go home!
Let's go home!"

Kayla just shook her head no.
That made the red fox mad.
He stomped his feet and said,

"Look little girl, I haven't eaten all day.
Give the bird to me or I'll take him myself!"

Just then the eagle
came out of hiding.
He grabbed the red
fox by the back of
the neck and flew off.
The red fox was
kicking and screaming,

"Please, please, please
let me go!"

The eagle flew over the lake to get
the fox away from Kayla and Peedy.

Kayla and Peedy are so happy!
They stop to dance because
the eagle saved them.

Now the cheetah was watching Kayla. The cheetah stared with his tongue hanging and wiggling from side to side out of his mouth. It looked like the cheetah finally found his dinner.

Then a strong wind appeared.
It was like a whirling tornado.
Everything was whirling,
twirling and flying around.

Kayla looked and saw,
the eagle was causing
the whirling wind.

The eagle continues to make the wind whirl until Kayla and Peedy are in the air.

Kayla and Peedy are having so much fun.

The cheetah **stared**, he **growled**. He was **mad**.

He screamed, "Bring back my dinner!
I'm a cheetah the world's fastest running animal.
I move faster than a jet plane but, I can't fly."

Meanwhile, Kayla's mother was calling,

"Kayla, Kayla, oh Kayla breakfast is ready."

Kayla was sitting up in her bed thinking

was that a dream? Peedy said,

" It's good to be home!

It's good to be home!"

Made in the USA
Columbia, SC
01 September 2021